Praise for *The P*

Longlisted for the DSC
Literature 2017

'*The Poison of Love*, an intense, dramatic novel written in a spare, well-crafted prose, delves into the most terrible, bitter, corrosive emotion that can pass off as love . . . K.R. Meera keeps a firm, economical grip on her words, and most sentences either express an emotion or move the narrative this way or that . . . A deep, dark tale'—*The Hindu*

'Enthralling . . . disturbing . . . A book that resonates powerfully with some of our most primal impulses—a consuming love, a corrosive hatred, a need for vengeance . . . What stands out the most in the novella is the sheer power of Meera's writing . . . Despite being translated from the original Malayalam, the book retains enough of its nuances and intensity, due in no small part to the commendable work done by translator Ministhy S., [especially] the universality of the imagery and emotions . . . From the horde of corpse-eating ants that trail across the pages of the book in increasingly large numbers—both literally and metaphorically—to the ravenous groups of feral monkeys that Tulsi fights with over food in Vrindavan, the images linger on in the minds of the reader in an insidious way . . . The key takeaway of the book [is] that [it] serves both as a warning against corrosive love and a passionate exploration of the very thing that it seeks to warn readers about'—*Indian Express*

'K.R. Meera's addictive latest novel follows the struggles of a young woman married to an incorrigible Lothario . . . Written with such breathless energy and foreboding that you can barely put the book down . . . Apart from Meera's obvious strengths as a novelist—economy, pace and strong characterisation—

she is also an expert plotter who could teach a thing or two to experienced crime writers, even . . . Almost every sentence either reveals something about the character or moves the action along. This, especially, is where she scores above a vast majority of literary novelists in India . . . *The Poison of Love* is a masterpiece in miniature and well worth your time'—*The Hindu Business Line*

'This slim novel stews in the passionate juice of wronged love . . . K.R. Meera's story, stripped to its bare essentials, sounds like a typical tale of love and betrayal, perhaps leading to an avenging fury with a knife, but something sets it apart from the reel life that throbs on TV screens or the pulp fiction genre . . . Intensity breathes through her style and every sentence is almost anguish . . . The plot seethes and twists like the Ganges by Mathura, with its banks lined with widows . . . A novella [of] so much intensity . . . Ministhy is new to translating K.R. Meera but manages to wring out each drop of obsession'—*Outlook*

'[A] searing love story . . . The brute force of [Meera's] plots, coupled with the irresistible perversity of her characters, make it easy to turn the pages of Meera's fiction . . . There is a sense of urgency in Meera's prose that is rare in any language . . . [Tulsi's] descent into black melancholy is the stuff of Greek tragedy (one is especially reminded of the venom of Euripides' *Medea*), but also all too human for its vulnerability and fragility'—*Huffington Post*

'The imagery that [Meera] uses is so intrinsic to the female experience, and to a sense of death and decay, themes that her stories are submerged in . . . *The Poison of Love* [is] an almost bestial exploration of a cruel love, and the madness for revenge that deforms the protagonist Tulsi . . . The personal never left her stories. Her heroines, Radhika, Tulsi, Chetna, even Prema from *The Gospel of Yudas*, seem to merge into one another in the way they encapsulate the condition of women'—*Mint*

to the theme but the prose itself, takes the protagonists out of themselves and into a sundered state of quasi-religious "ecstasy" (in the original sense of standing outside oneself). A power not unlike that of the saint Meera's poetry, or indeed that of the poems of a John Donne'—*Wire*

'Love and revenge with a feminist flavour . . . The nucleus of K.R. Meera's oeuvre is obsessive love, and her protagonists give themselves over to it completely—and often to their complete detriment. This is where her writing differs from all versions of the same tales, which are made to seem like nothing but cautionary ones. Her heroines claim their emotions, and the consequences of having them, instead of allowing themselves to be merely victims of circumstance. Despite being set in a disturbing psychic realm, *The Poison of Love*'s feminist politics are taut . . . There's a reason why it's the simplest stories that get told, over and over again. Despite the macabre details of *The Poison of Love*, its fundamental premise of betrayal and longing are resoundingly familiar'—*Open*

'There are undercurrents of Greek tragedy . . . [Meera] shows political, religious and domestic violence as leaving equally deep scars on the body and soul of [a] woman . . . Meera is an expert plotter, each sentence reveals something new about the character and moves the action along, but nowhere can you anticipate what is coming next. Ministhy S.'s translation from the original Malayalam evokes the breathless energy of Meera's writing . . . Love, Meera shows, is the other great equalizer besides death. She blurs the line separating love and death by presenting both to be forces that bring out the suppressed perversity of human feelings'—*Telegraph*

'*The Poison of Love* is an ode to loss and suffering . . . Instead, it presents a world of violence, physical and emotional . . . Brace for a rollercoaster ride'—*Financial Express*

'No one writes about searing love like K.R. Meera does, and this novel proves it again'—*Scroll*

Praise for *The Gospel of Yudas*

'Without veering away from the singular plot of a young woman's obsessive quest for dangerous love, it manages all at once to capture the aftermath of police brutality, the macabre face of the state machinery, the price of betrayal and the blind sense of sacrifice that makes some young men and women decide to give up their lives for the sake of a promised revolution . . . A skilful achievement . . . Meera's lyrical and luminous prose must be singled out for praise. She effortlessly transports the reader to the lush forests and picturesque riversides of Kerala with as much aplomb as she describes the torture of captured Naxalites. The book also brings alive the political history of Kerala . . . *The Gospel of Yudas* is a lesson in compactness. It succeeds in showing how the oft-neglected genre of the novella, when executed by an expert hand, can claim its legitimate space in the world of literature . . . The new translation by Rajesh Rajamohan does not disappoint . . . I found the translation smooth and grounded, allowing the reader to delve into the story without a moment's hesitation about a language that does not belong'—Meena Kandasamy, *The Hindu*

'A new English translation of award-winning Malayalam writer K.R. Meera's novella, *The Gospel of Yudas*, is a reminder of the horror of that period, of just how deranged the violence became and the effects it had on ordinary lives . . . *The Gospel of Yudas* is revolutionary literature. Meera reminds us that the Emergency was not an accident of history but the logical outcome of State machinery deployed a certain way. Those brave enough to fight the State suffer terribly so that the rest of us don't have to. What we owe them is to fix their sacrifice in our memory, in public consciousness . . . *The Gospel of Yudas* is really the Passion of Christ, a story of suffering redeemed by love. The love in this short, intense book is damaged, even broken. But it's love all the same'—*India Today*

'Takes its readers through a perfect journey into the hot, sticky, messy, grimy underbelly of human emotion . . . This is not a romance novel; this is a novel about the dirty, grimy, painful and black emotions of love and loss. It sucks a reader in with its calm writing only to drown her in a tidal wave of human honesty'—*Hindustan Times*

'*The Gospel of Yudas* is a moving story that opens up an ethical discourse on issues of evil, good, guilt and redemption . . . [It] powerfully illustrates the fine line between love, revolution, power, violence and the price one pays for idealism'—*Free Press Journal*

'Being mesmerised, so that you don't want to escape, and constantly aware of other layers beyond the one you're engaged with . . . such can also be the effect of reading K.R. Meera's strange, compelling novel *The Gospel of Yudas* . . . A disquieting book, its off-kilter quality coming from its mixing of conventional narrative with allegory, hard politics with abstractions about human lives and desires . . . evocative'—Jai Arjun Singh, *Scroll*

'Meera's work . . . is lush in violence and metaphor'—*Open*

Praise for *Hangwoman*

'Meera is at her best when she examines the lives of her women characters . . . The writing is strong . . . An epic novel'—*Outlook*

'A daring book, for the panoramic sweep of its canvas, for the sheer audacity of its narrative logic . . . for its irreverent play with the paradoxes of life—Love and Death'—*The Hindu*

'This striking novel includes within its majestic sweep the enigmas of the human condition . . . Stunning images bring out the depth and intensity of Chetna's spiritual development, and stand testimony to the author's consummate writing style'—*Deccan Herald*

'Meera achieves a vision of [Kolkata] that is both acutely observed, almost anthropological, in its minute detailing and, at the same time, mythic in its evocation of the city's decaying, decrepit majesty . . . One of the most extraordinary accomplishments in recent Indian fiction'—*Indian Express*

'An absorbing novel'—*New Indian Express*

'One of the strongest voices in contemporary Malayalam literature . . . Meera plays with the reader's anticipation masterfully . . . The novel is extremely atmospheric . . . Meera turns the entire city into a haunted house'—*Open*

'The book heaves with violence, is lush with metaphor and shocks with details. The reader can only gasp at the surgical precision with which Meera describes the act of hanging'—*The Hindu Business Line*

'An immense, intense coiled rope of a novel . . . There are chillingly clear-eyed vignettes and moments of razor-sharp dark humour . . . If *Aarachar*, the original, was—plot, stock and barrel—"Malayalam's ultimate gift of love to Bengal," as its translator J. Devika puts it, its English translation is no less a bonus for showing us, its non-Malayali, non-Bengali readership, the dazzling interstices of her story, instantly recognisable across time and space'—*India Today*

'An incisive critique of the barbarism of the death penalty . . . [The book] gives us a glimpse into the inner lives of those who have been deputed to execute it through generations . . . A vast and riveting sweep of time, locked into the gritty interstices of the contemporary—a pastiche made of fact and fiction, news bulletins and nightmares'—*Mint*

'Stunning . . . Meera weaves history, romance and the politics of the present together into a narrative of incredible complexity . . . J. Devika's translation is superb, and she captures the rich detail of Meera's Malayalam: descriptive, textured and evocative . . . Reading Meera, in Devika's meticulous and inspired translation, we experience the author's spectacular ventriloquism. And we are also reminded of the tradition that Meera comes from, which she has burnished and transcended with her epic novel'—*Caravan*

Praise for *Yellow Is the Colour of Longing*

'Interesting, challenging'—Mahasweta Devi

'[Meera's] stories cover an amazing range, and in each her idiom is inseparable from the plots and characters . . . Each story invokes the inner violence of contemporary society in Kerala'—*Caravan*

'One of the most powerful voices in contemporary Malayalam writing'—*Mint*

'A literary heavyweight'—*Indian Express*

PENGUIN BOOKS
THE POISON OF LOVE

K.R. Meera is a multi-award-winning writer and journalist. She has published short stories, novels and essays, and has won some of the most prestigious literary prizes including the Kerala Sahitya Akademi Award, the Vayalar Award and the Odakkuzhal Award. In 2015, she won the Kendra Sahitya Akademi Award for *Aarachar*, widely hailed as a contemporary classic and published by Penguin Random House India as *Hangwoman*. In 2017, her *The Poison of Love* was published to ecstatic acclaim. She lives in Kottayam with her husband Dileep and daughter Shruthi.

Ministhy S. is an IAS officer who hails from Kerala and works in Uttar Pradesh. She is also a writer and translator. Her translation of K.R. Meera's *The Poison of Love* has been widely lauded as a masterpiece. Her books in English include essay collections and books for children. She has also translated books from Hindi and English to Malayalam.

The Poison of Love

K.R. MEERA

Translated from the Malayalam by
MINISTHY S.

PENGUIN BOOKS
An imprint of Penguin Random House

PENGUIN BOOKS

USA | Canada | UK | Ireland | Australia
New Zealand | India | South Africa | China

Penguin Books is part of the Penguin Random House group of companies
whose addresses can be found at global.penguinrandomhouse.com

Published by Penguin Random House India Pvt. Ltd
7th Floor, Infinity Tower C, DLF Cyber City,
Gurgaon 122 002, Haryana, India

First published in Malayalam as *Meerasadhu* by DC Books, Kottayam 2008
First published in Hamish Hamilton by Penguin Random House India 2017
Published in Penguin Books in 2018

Copyright © K.R. Meera 2008, 2017
English translation copyright © Ministhy S. 2017

ISBN 9780143442721

Typeset in Adobe Caslon Pro by Manipal Digital Systems, Manipal
Printed at Thomson Press India Ltd, New Delhi

www.penguin.co.in

Dedicated to
All the Meeras of Vrindavan

The Poison of Love

Love is like milk. With the passage of time, it sours, splits and becomes poison.

Madhav gave me that poison. I did not die; instead I killed him. I, the widow, came to Mathura's Vrindavan. That was twelve years ago.

On the very first day, old Ghanshyam Pandit, a retired schoolteacher sporting a tilak on his forehead, had pointed to the old women with shaven heads, hobbling along slowly—walking stick in one hand and tiffin carrier in the other—through gullies reeking of manure and urine, girdled by five thousand temples, and introduced them thus: 'Madam, look at these women. Haven't you heard of Bhakt Meera? The devotee of Lord Krishna who wrote Meera bhajans. These are refugees, widows. We call them Meera sadhus. They sit in the bhajanmandap from dawn to dusk and recite the name of Krishna. That is their sole work. They get a daily allowance of two and a half rupees. Some milk, ten grams of rice and

3

dal. Pitiable creatures! The contributions of Krishna devotees like you are their only succour. If you wish you may donate to the temple trust.'

Something shattered inside me as I stared at the women. Feeling dizzy, I followed Ghanshyam Pandit up a flight of winding stairs. A dim green signboard—the word 'Dharamsala' written on it in Hindi—hung above a narrow door. I was horrified when I entered. There was a sea of shaven heads. Reverberating, incessant crying, as if someone was being strangled—Hare Rama, Hare Rama, Rama Rama, Hare Hare . . . Hare Krishna, Hare Krishna, Krishna Krishna Hare Hare . . . Outside, the afternoon sun was subdued. Disoriented, I started confusing the faces of the human beings with those of the animals moving relentlessly on the streets. It was a dirty hall with more stone pillars than were required. Right in the middle, a Radha–Govind statue draped in yellow silks and garlanded with marigolds stood on a small pedestal. Seeping in through the window bars, the weak sunlight gleamed on the shaven heads. Faces filled with pathos. Skinny bodies. Tarnished eye glasses. The smell of dried flowers, soiled old clothes and sweat. The sound of broken hearts.

4

I caressed my shaven head. I felt I was Meera too. Indeed, in reality, I was Meera.

That evening, I met the temple trust in-charge and requested permission to join as a Meera sadhu. I bought a stick. Also a tiffin carrier made of aluminium. After a ritual bath in the Yamuna, I went to the Maighar with my stick and bowl. Thus, I too became a Meera sadhu.

Everybody addressed me as 'Mai'. I too woke up at the crack of dawn, bathed in the Yamuna, smeared sandalwood paste on my forehead, shouted 'Bolo Krishna Krishna Jai,' and shuffled through the streets with the aid of the stick. In the scorching summer, in the torrential rains, in the biting winter that froze the bark on the trees, I vengefully begged in front of the Govind Dev temple. I fought with monkeys for the fruits thrown by visitors. Hitting them and throwing stones at them, I made those monkeys my foes. The wounds I sustained during these scuffles became badly infected and hurt grievously. The pain delighted me.

From morning till afternoon, I sat on the bhajanmandap, chanting 'Krishna Krishna Hare Hare,' forgetting myself. I fumed as I prayed. I stood in front of the Rangji temple, grinding my teeth.

I will love that man. With bitter resentment, I will love him. In my hollow heart, I shall safeguard that beat of revenge to ensure his destruction. I shall emit the agony of bones falling off. I will hunt him until death—and beyond. When he attempts to kiss another woman, he shall be smashed to smithereens.

Twelve years. Twelve years of waiting. He came at last—just as I had known he would. Madhav. My husband. My bitterest enemy. My only man. The father of my two children. Stricken on one side of his body, a red Kashmiri shawl draped over his white shirt, he came hobbling and limping. I raised my hood like a king cobra to receive him. My tongue thirsted for blood. Shock spread like poison across his chiselled face. He is very handsome. Compassionate eyes. A sharp, high-bridged nose. When he laughs, a cute cleft appears on his chin. He gazed at me as if I were a spirit. My missing front teeth, sunken eyes, skinny bag of a body, my tonsured head and torn sari. To complete my vengeance, I crawled on my knees towards him and thrust my begging bowl at him. 'Please give something to this forlorn soul, mahashay!'

He lost control then and cried out, 'Tulsi!'

I stopped beseeching. I smiled innocently, exposing my toothless gums. 'Tulsi is dead, Madhav mahashay. I am Meera . . . Meera sadhu.'

This is that story. The autobiography of a Meera sadhu.

ONE

In principle, love and spirit are but one. Both ache to break free from fetters and take possession of suitable bodies.

I shall start the story on the day Madhav appeared in Vrindavan. Seeing me, he clutched his chest and collapsed. A few people carried him off somewhere. The bells of the Rangji temple had been ringing for a while. It was time for the darshan.

Holding up my sari by its hem, begging bowl and stick in hand, I rushed along with the other women to get ahead in the queue. After the darshan, I jostled for a share of the annadanam being doled out: one dry roti and some cooked vegetables. Then I swept the top floor of the Govind Dev temple. I threw bananas for the monkeys. In the evening, I collected my daily ration from the temple trust—ten grams of rice, dal—and ten rupees as allowance. After the night darshan of Banke Bihari, I returned to the Maighar. On the way, I sang a Meera bhajan.

'Some mock me for being tainted by the Cloud-coloured One's love. Some shower praises. As for me, I am enchanted by my own songs and travel with the saints . . .'

The next day, when Ramakrishna Pandit of the temple trust informed me that Madhav had been admitted in the speciality hospital at Vrindavan, I just sat lazily by Nidhivan—the grass hut entwined with jasmine creepers in front of the Rangji temple. The place where Radha and Krishna are supposed to meet. No one is allowed to enter the area at night. That is my usual begging place, near the cluster of dried jasmines. Just for fun, of course. As they make love, invisible to the rest of us, let Radha and Govinda be vexed by a beggar woman's voice! I loathe every love story except my own.

When the gravelled pathway burns in summer, I walk barefoot on it. The body is the raw material for both love and devotion. When the soles of my feet erupt in blisters, I remember Madhav. The first time he had held me close, his body had burned more furiously than that. Back then, I had regarded myself with more esteem than now.

'Meera mai . . . Who is that babu admitted in the hospital? He wants to see you.'

The pandit came near, wiping the red spittle of paan off his lips.

'Which babu, Panditji? In Meera's Vrindavan, there is only one Babu. The rest are all women.'

'He is a famous journalist. Your relative, perhaps?'

'I have only one relative . . .' I bowed before him, smiling ingenuously, and then hobbled out with the help of my stick.

Madhav wants to see me.

I was seventeen the first time he saw me. Back then I was an IIT student. Madhav was a correspondent with an English magazine in Chennai. He had come to the campus to prepare a report on the psychological pressures faced by the students at IIT. Vinay had introduced us—and Madhav's large eyes, framed by long eyelashes, had searched mine for something ineffable. Though he did not look into my eyes again for the rest of that meeting, choosing instead to indulge in polite talk, he made me acutely aware of my womanhood.

Madhav's report was published the following week. The article mentioned my name. He sent me a few copies. Soon after, Vinay was selected during campus recruitment and went to the USA. Madhav would call me occasionally. We started meeting each other. He always talked in a charming manner. He made me laugh a lot. Whenever I sat next to him, I felt within my usually empty heart something akin to milk, which rose bubbling to the surface as it boiled, and spilled over when we separated. My heart was left desolate. I longed to see him again. Madhav started writing to me. The length of his letters increased as the years passed. Madhav wrote openly and uninhibitedly about the twenty-seven lovers who had been part of his life. I was left totally shocked.

'I never went seeking anyone. All of them came in search of me.'

Thus Madhav justified himself when we met. 'Each woman comes and having played her role, as if in a drama, leaves the stage. I simply cannot find what I am actually looking for . . . I have tried to discover the object of my search. Whatever it may be, it is definitely not sex, Tulsi.'

I had stared at him in amazement. Madhav was a strikingly handsome man, even back then— with the cleft in his chin, his big eyes and sharp, prominent nose. But good looks alone cannot arouse love in a woman. I wondered about this often, delved deep into what accounted for his irresistible charm. The meticulous care he takes in even the minutest details. His jokes—untold by others. Perhaps that was it.

I passed my engineering examinations and took my degree. Madhav had, by then, become a renowned journalist in Delhi.

My father decided to get me married off before I began my higher studies. When he learned this, Madhav had jumped on a flight to Thiruvananthapuram.

'Tulsi, this is nonsense.'

Madhav was furious. His anger perplexed me. Marriage was inevitable, after all. My mother's uterine cancer had progressed to the third stage. She was hurrying to offer her three daughters—Tulsi, Tamara and Mallika—at the feet of three suitable bridegrooms.

Madhav refused to listen to anything.

'Tulsi, it is stupid to get married at this age. I remember what your teachers said. You were their most promising student. Someone who could be India's pride! Possibly a future Nobel Prize winner!'

I blushed. I felt great about myself. When he heard that Vinay was to be my bridegroom, Madhav's face fell. 'Tulsi and Vinay do not match each other,' he raged, going on to deliver a tirade about love and marriage. 'A marriage without mutual attraction is futile. It is like throwing your life down forcefully and watching it disintegrate.'

'I like Vinay,' I argued. 'And Vinay likes me.'

'That is not enough for marriage,' Madhav bristled. 'Do you long to see him when you are apart? Crave his voice when you are alone? When you see him, do you yearn to clasp him to your heart? Do you feel as if your heart is brimming over? And when you leave him, does the world seem bleak, empty?'

'I am not a silly romantic.'

'That is because you haven't experienced true love.'

His long eyelashes caressed me as if with peacock feathers. I became distressed and gloomy. Eager to change the topic, I inquired about his girlfriend.

Madhav smiled. 'Ah, we have parted ways. All my relationships till now were in vain. It's only now that I have found the one I was searching for.'

When I asked who it was, he took hold of my hand.

'Am I less eligible than Vinay?'

That was totally unexpected. I blushed. To hide my surprise, I laughed aloud. 'It is not an issue of eligibility. Oh, indeed no, I could never love you. When I look at you, I see a room full of women right behind you. Twenty-seven in all. And you, resplendent amidst them—Krishna of Vrindavan . . .'

The shadow of humiliation darkened Madhav's face. 'Tulsi, I shall never refuse any woman's love. It would devastate her. If my love can make a woman happy, why would I want to deny her? You do not understand, Tulsi. They were all unhappy. They had never been loved. They had been denied love by fathers, husbands or sweethearts. I offered them my love as alms. This body of mine will be eaten up by ants and worms one day. If it can be of use to another human being, why should I refuse? But be clear about this—I never desired any of them. I never demanded anything from them either. But you are different. For the first time, I long for a woman.'

Silence spread between us. At first I felt rebellious, and then it changed to an indulgent affection. But my face remained impassive. When we parted, he looked at me in an accusatory way. 'Love has one fault, Tulsi.

If you let go, it will fall. It will shatter on the ground. You should not let go.'

I became nervous. There was an inkling of pain in his eyes. He left without saying goodbye. Still, he participated in the engagement ceremony. He helped my father with the arrangements—reserving the hall and booking the vehicles. On one of those days, he called up and requested in a pleading voice, 'Tulsi, stay my friend forever.' Just a friend, at least, he reiterated.

My hands, holding the phone, had trembled. Waves of heat and cold passed through my body at once. *Madhav loved me.* It felt like a joke. The woman he had found after twenty-seven lovers! With a tremor of fear, I realized that I was experiencing all the symptoms of love that he had spoken of— for Madhav, not Vinay. I was yearning to see *him*. I wanted to talk to *him* when I was alone. My heart brimmed over whenever I met *him* and felt drained when *he* went away.

My mind became fickle. When I tried to desire Vinay, it ran like a monkey towards Madhav. He transformed into an omnipresent figure in my life. He became my father's trusted aide. My mother's pet. My sisters' favourite buddy. He accompanied us to Chennai and Bangalore to select the sari and the jewellery for the wedding. Whenever he came near me, I felt uncomfortable. Even more so when he went away from me. A time bomb ticked away within my heart.

I waited impatiently for the day when Vinay would arrive. Only he could save me. Turn me into the old Tulsi once again. But Vinay was oblivious to everything. He did not even bother to look into my eyes, as I stood waiting for him at the airport. He spoke only about green cards and visas.

Madhav called me every night. With false enthusiasm, he spoke about the best tailoring shops and the latest jewellery designs. He went searching for a shade of nail polish to complement my aquamarine wedding sari, scouring almost all the shops in town.

'Blue sari and blouse with a diamond necklace and earrings, right? I am imagining you as a bride, Tulsi.'

'Why imagine? You can see for yourself on the day of the wedding.'

'I forgot to tell you that. I will not be there for the ceremony. I must leave the morning before your wedding . . .'

19

'That's unfair . . .'

'Do not insist, Tulsi. I will not come.' Madhav's voice was firm.

I disconnected the call, not knowing what to say. I felt a strange anxiety. To find refuge, I tried Vinay's number.

'Vinay, I felt like talking to you.' My voice was trembling uncontrollably.

Vinay yawned. 'Talk? At this time? Goodness! Are you mad?'

I became weak and cowardly. 'Go to sleep, Tulsi,' he said. 'We have a lifetime ahead for talking. Once we reach the US, we will be left to ourselves. You can talk to me till you tire of me.'

I tired of him in that very instant. I hung up with numbing frustration. My nerves were frayed and I was filled with disappointment. The prospect of my marriage with Vinay filled me with dread. Vinay was definitely not the right person. But I became helpless on seeing my parents' faces full of fervent hope.

Two days before my wedding, on an afternoon when my mother had gone for her medical check-up, Madhav entered the drawing room where my sister Mallika and I were sitting and chatting. He had a bottle of blue nail polish. Without asking for my permission, he sat down on the floor and started applying nail polish on my toenails. Mallika burst into laughter. When I resisted, he held my feet together firmly. 'Sit there quietly,' he ordered.

It was the first time anyone had touched my feet. My head felt light. Madhav continued his task diligently. He asked for some water. When Mallika went to the kitchen, Madhav took my feet into his hands and looked at me. 'Feet like lotus buds,' he murmured. His eyes were moist. His tears were real, as were his trembling lips. I felt dizzy. He rubbed his face on my feet and kissed them. His tears were on my feet. It seemed unreal, as if I was bereft of my senses.

'Has Vinay ever kissed you like this?' he asked me with pity. I felt a sinking sense of inferiority.

'Do you think he will ever kiss you like this?' He stood up and, taking my face into his hands, looked into my eyes. 'My kisses are my offerings to you. You should not refuse them. Vinay cannot kiss like me. He does not know how to love like me. Mark my words—you will regret it. You will cry for having rejected me. There is time yet.' Madhav pressed his lips to my cheeks. Caressed my neck adoringly. 'There is time yet . . . but very little.'

I pushed him away and ran into the next room. I thought I had died.

There is time yet.

Even after twenty years, I could hear that voice clearly. After twenty years, I could still recall his touch.

His touch was magical, spellbinding. It was as if I was in a trance. Like a gopika enchanted with Krishna's divine flute music, I lost awareness of the world around me. My body was under some sort of black magic. I was thrown off balance.

I called Vinay and told him, 'I do not want this marriage.'

'Tulsi, are you mad?' Vinay was furious.

'We are not right for each other,' I persevered stubbornly.

'Too late,' he mocked.

When he angrily cut the call, I felt crushed again.

'This marriage will not work,' I told my father too.

My father laughed: 'This is the result of our over-indulgence!'

No one heard me out. No one gave me strength. Every refuge fell apart.

That night, I called Madhav. 'I will come,' I said. I was panting.

'Ah,' he let out a deep breath. 'Take a bath and get ready by three. The car will come at four near the gate at the back. We will tie the mangalsutra at five in the Devi temple.'

'Mangalsutra?'

I was dumbfounded. Madhav's subdued laughter trickled through the phone.

'Tulsi, I was sure that you would come. I have already purchased the mangalsutra and the garlands, and paid the wedding fees at the temple. I have also booked two seats on the eight a.m. flight to Delhi. Everything has been arranged.'

Cruelly taunting everyone—my mother who was on her deathbed, my proud father who had never bowed his head before anyone, my two sisters and Vinay—I eloped the next morning.

Even after being estranged for twelve years, I have to confess one fact: Madhav is the only man in my Vrindavan. Not merely because he was my husband for eight years or that he fathered my two children. No one else could make me love so passionately.

Having met Madhav again after twelve years, lying in that dilapidated room in the Maighar, I remembered everything. I travelled, jolting in the horse-carriage of memories. The street lamp behind the Madan Mohan temple blazed intensely outside my window. The silent, deserted street evoked rapture in me. I felt the urge to pick up the tanpura and dance and sing on the top floor of the Govind Dev temple. I am the sweeper woman of the temple. The key to the staircase is with me. You can see all of Vrindavan from the third storey. I have sung Meera bhajans and danced up there. Meera bhajan.

'Meera beseeches thus: Cloud-coloured One, please pull this small boat on to that distant shore. Stop this relentless coming and going.'

I wanted to see Madhav again. It was unbelievable how my body was aroused by his presence. For twelve years, we had not seen, talked to or touched each other. I fantasized about making love to him once more. I would remove my stinking sari and the old underclothes, and stand in front of him—all skin and bones. I would scratch my shaven head hideously, shamelessly reveal my pathetic, drooping breasts, my wretched thighs shorn of any fat, my bent and bowed back, my calloused, dirty feet with the toenails digging in. I would teach him the meaning of beauty. With love, I would purify him too.

TWO

My love was like a serpent that had swallowed its own tail. It twisted around in circles, trying to consume itself. The hunger never abated. The mouth never became free. However, it boosted my self-esteem. Once, my self-esteem was what I had felt for myself. But having fallen in love with Madhav, it had become synonymous with being adored and valued by him.

When Nabaneeta shuffled into the room after finishing the daily routine, I was still lying there.

'Your famous relative is still in the hospital, Tulsi mai,' she said. 'The temple trustee has asked you to visit him.'

I conjured Madhav's stricken form in my mind's eye. When I laughed cruelly, the rust-ridden cot creaked vigorously.

'Trustee? Which trustee? There is only one trustee in Vrindavan, Nabaneeta mai. That is Shri Krishna!'

At night, when Chameli and Nabaneeta fell asleep, I stayed awake. After many years, here was a night when I could have slept really well had I wished to.

The Maighar was a dilapidated building. If you stretched your arms to the side, they would hit the walls of the narrow corridor. On either side were rooms, barely two hundred square feet, shared by three women. The daily rent was five rupees. At the time of my arrival, the rent had been a rupee, and the daily allowance two and a half rupees.

I had got this cot after paying five thousand rupees each to both Ghanshyam Pandit and the temple trustee Ramakrishna Pandit. That was twelve years ago. In the February of 1995. On my birthday. The ninetieth day after I had let go of the kids. The second day after I was discharged from the psychiatry ward of Thiruvananthapuram Medical College.

I had reached home from the hospital in my father's car. The ageing inspector general of police had looked utterly defeated and shorn of his dignity. I had covertly watched my father dry his tears. That night, I had called up a travel agency and booked a flight to Delhi. Early the next morning, I stole two or three wads of hundred-rupee notes from my father's cupboard and sneaked away to Delhi yet again. I took a taxi to the hotel and checked in. Then, at the familiar beauty parlour, I demanded a tonsure.

'What are you saying?' the beautician had asked, astounded, as she gathered my long, black, glistening hair into her hands. 'Such lovely tresses!'

'I want to be free.'

'It will never be the same again.'

'Nothing will ever be the same again.' I yawned.

Helpless, she had started cutting my hair. Like dead snakes, long, glittering streams of hair had fallen to the ground. My head felt like a balloon tied to a thread. It yearned to fly aloft.

I had walked aimlessly through Ashoka Road. The cool wind tickled my shaven head. I caressed it often. I had never been loved by anyone to the full extent of my desire. No one had cried, heartbroken, over me. I had become a nonentity, an emptiness, in my thirtieth year of living. Like a burst balloon, my life had become irrelevant. Maybe every woman's fate was the same.

In that mood, I might even have loved the beggar who approached from the opposite side. If only he had looked at me the way Madhav used to, if he had smiled at me like Madhav had, uttered even a single word as softly as Madhav had. In that dim sunlight, I stood on the path, staring at a tree in full bloom, my tonsured head freezing in the cold February wind.

Thinking of the ephemeral nature of spring, I felt anger towards the tree; and then, thinking of possibly being reborn as one, I also felt hatred towards it. What a disaster that would be! Someone would break off my branches. Woodpeckers and parasitic creepers would hurt me. I would have to contain the retribution within myself. If I were a tree, I would curse my way to blooming and shed my leaves with a vengeance. I would fill my flowers with poison. Butterflies and bees would drop dead along with the dried leaves. In my next birth too I would destroy everything.

It was then that I had seen the board of the Tourist Travels bus service to Agra via Mathura. The word 'Mathura' touched the memory of Madhav, which was hidden, like an iron nail driven deep into my flesh. The wound started bleeding. Breathing hard, I made my way to the hotel. There too they had displayed the timings of trains and buses to prominent tourist destinations, along with the taxi rates. Again, I saw 'Mathura' there.

When I lay alone that night, my mad frenzy began again. I saw Madhav wherever I looked. Why had he accepted me without love? What had I been to him? I was an earthen pot, used and thrown away.

It had shattered. The pieces had scattered in different directions. It would never again recover its original form nor regain its identity. It would never again get to know fullness.

In order to help me sleep, I ordered vodka. Before I discovered the truths about Madhav, I had hated alcohol. I felt light-headed after drinking—as though I had just got my head shaved. I did not remember my birthday then. Neither did I decide on the journey to Mathura. But sometime in the night, I had a dream—a loathsome one.

I dreamed of the Salem mango tree that grew south of my ancestral home which had been sold off long ago. I had returned to its deserted and silent shade, exhausted and drowsy. The sight of the splendid mango blossoms filled me with joy. Suddenly, causing the earth to quake, a monstrous black snake slithered down from amidst the mango blooms. Partly uncoiling itself, it began to swing menacingly from a low branch. The tip of its black tail reached my feet. It raised its three-hooded head that was as huge as an elephant's, and reared it as high as the house itself. The middle hood was white. The three forked tongues flicked out blood red, splayed fearsomely against the sky.

Horror-struck, I ran to the east of the house where my children were playing. Gathering them close to my heart, I cowered in terror inside the cowshed. The younger one wriggled out of my arms and scampered towards the mango tree. Screaming 'Kanna!' I raced desperately after him. The next scene was terrible. As if an anthill had erupted, innumerable rat-sized monkeys appeared, and savagely attacked the snake, mauling it to death. The serpent struggled in its death throes, flailing and thrashing its three hoods. My intrepid young son reached out to touch a monkey. The monkey turned its head and snarled with irritation, blue blood dripping from its mouth.

I had woken up crying 'Kanna!' in terror.

I was trembling even after waking. Everything had seemed real except for Kanna. *Except Kanna.* He was not there to call out 'Amma!' Yet the scream—'Kanna!'—rolled about loudly in my skull, clattering incessantly like a coin in a misshapen begging bowl.

I could not go back to sleep that night. I felt disoriented from the alcohol. As I tossed and turned restlessly in bed, I resolutely decided to travel the next day. Travel can exorcise the restlessness of the spirit, as well as that of love.

In the two-and-a-half-hour train journey to Mathura, I slept, standing amidst the milling crowd. I dreamed of Madhav. We were eloping again. We embraced hurriedly and looked deeply into each other's eyes. I was drawn into Madhav's large eyes framed by those long eyelashes. Whatever had occurred till then felt like a passing nightmare. Madhav enveloped me like a warm cloud. 'We will go to Mathura,' Madhav murmured, as on the night of our marriage. His moustache gently tickled my ears. I giggled. When I finally opened my eyes, I saw myself—head shaven, dressed in a loose shirt and ill-fitting jeans, giggling. I felt utterly ridiculous. As in my waking life, in my sleep too, Madhav had made me feel ridiculous.

Twelve years ago, the fare from Mathura railway station to Vrindavan had been fifty rupees. I had hired a tonga. It was a difficult journey. Dust rose all along the rutted roads that stretched over ugly landscapes. The horse had plodded along lazily, a black cloth tied across its eyes. The tonga driver called out, 'Madhuban,' and pointed at a clump of thorny trees. Reflecting on the Madhuban of my fantasies, I laughed with self-loathing. The tonga stopped by the side of a drain in a small town. Bleak monuments stood all around me. It was a dismal street full of small shops. When the driver said, 'Memsahib, we have reached Vrindavan,' I had again felt the sharp sting of betrayal. *Lies! Everything was a lie! Krishna, Yamuna, Kalindi, Vrindavan, Ambady, Kadamba forests—all of them.* To comprehend the truth, one had to traverse infeasible distances—to places of no return.

It was the tonga driver who introduced me to Ghanshyam Pandit. 'A guide who knew English.' The pandit showed me around Vrindavan. He wore a long, white khadi shirt and baggy pyjamas. There was a long tilak on his forehead. 'There are more than five thousand temples here,' he said. 'There are no houses in Vrindavan. Every house is a temple. Krishna exists in every grain of this place.' While he pointed out the south Indian-style minaret of the Ranganath temple, Seva Kunj and the thicket of starry wild jasmines, I meditated on ways of seeking revenge. I had not wished to stay on in Vrindavan even then. But at the Govind Dev temple I got a devastating shock.

In the sixteenth century, using the red marble contributed by Akbar, Raja Man Singh had the seven-storeyed temple built, spending more than a crore rupees. Later, Aurangzeb attacked it. The top four storeys of the temple had been destroyed. Now the temple stands desolate. There is no idol to worship there. From a distance, the red monument with its countless pillars appeared haunted. In the top floors, groups of pigeons and mynahs flapped about frantically. I felt a sense of déjà vu—the greyish sunlight of summer, the innumerable pillars, the red-hued darkness inside, the bleak emptiness. I scratched my tonsured head. In that instant, a most unexpected event occurred. A troop of monkeys appeared. Just as in my nightmare—innumerous monkeys! I screamed out in terror.

'They are the consorts of Krishna, madam. Do not be afraid,' Ghanshyam Pandit consoled me. I remembered my children as I followed him, breathing heavily. My mind started wandering. The guide explained that it would bring good fortune if one were to travel from Rameshwaram to Kashi via Vrindavan. He led me further to a building constructed with marble slabs on which the names and addresses of people had been carved, as on tombstones. 'Radha Ballabh statue is now situated here, madam.'

I gazed at the numerous marble slabs.

'Your name too can be carved here, madam. Give some contribution to the trust.'

If someone gave fifty thousand rupees, the names of everyone in their family would be carved here, he elaborated. That money was meant for the refugees. I felt like laughing. I strolled inside lazily, scratching my shaven head. Suddenly, the laughter vanished. My legs froze.

On the sopanam, the holy steps leading to the sanctum sanctorum, stood the statue of the Kalasarpa, the glistening black king cobra, its head reared high. I stared at it—it was the serpent from my nightmare. Its dark body had an oily shimmer all over. Of its three hoods, the middle one was pure white. The forked tongues were red as blood. Krishna played his flute beneath the splayed hoods. I almost went berserk.

It was later that I saw the Meera sadhus and even later that I remembered my birthday. The widows returning to their rooms after darshan and annadanam had reminded me of ants scuffling along with their white eggs. Their faces resembled lamps that had died out, bereft of oil. Empty lives. On that birthday, I decided to be reborn as Meera.

When I asked for permission to become a Meera sadhu, Ramakrishna Pandit, the temple trustee, had looked at me compassionately. He was chewing paan.

'What is the need for you to do it? You are so young. So beautiful . . .'

'I am a widow,' I said stubbornly.

'Go back home, child.'

'I have no home.'

'We will give your photograph to the police. They will trace your home.'

'I will complain that you tried to harass me.'

'See, all the places are full . . . Mathura is known as the city of widows . . . Unofficially, there are ten thousand . . . No vacant places . . .'

'One more being added to the ten thousand, or subtracted from it—what difference does it make? I have to be accommodated somehow.'

I took out a bundle of hundred-rupee notes from the bag.

'Are you some sort of criminal?'

'My father was an inspector general in Kerala.'

The Pandit looked thoughtfully at me.

'It will be very tough here,' he forewarned. 'A woman born in a good family, like you, could never adjust to it.'

'I have no family,' I said. 'My spouse is Krishna. My home is Vrindavan. From now on, my life will be here. My death too.'

I am obstinate. Finally, he gave in and I joined the ten thousand. I washed the clothes of the Meera sadhus. I took care of them, prepared food, took them by the hand for the darshan. I swept clean all three floors of the Govind Dev temple. I cleaned the pathways of the Rangji temple. Everything was an offering to Madhav. Flower offerings of retribution.

The bells at Rangji temple rang out then, snapping me out of my reverie, and ushering in the three o'clock rituals. I went to the Yamuna to wash the soiled clothes of Nabaneeta and Chameli. A sanyasi dozed on the rocks, dazed with marijuana. The cold wind blew its flute rapaciously. I stepped into the waters. The black waves slithered and coiled sinuously around my feet.

The Yamuna is a Meera sadhu too. With her waters drying up, she is withered and shrivelled; curling up to sleep with a bowed back, her bones jutting out. Pretending devotion, unclean men wash away their dirt in her.

I hummed a Meera bhajan.

'Lord, a heartbroken Meera waits for you by the riverside, every night. Just to catch a glimpse . . .'

I remembered Madhav. My wounds became furiously aroused. I wanted to see him. I wanted to cross his threshold, clutching my stick. '*Jeete raho, mahashay . . . Jeete raho! To steal more clothes, to break more mud pots, to make love to more gopikas, stay eternally alive!*' I wanted to bless him thus.

Vengeance started inflaming my mind. It raged against my own self. Swallowing my tail, my hunger was snuffed out.

THREE

Madhav's love was an acid that corroded the vessel itself. My flesh burned, my bones melted. I dissolved into him entirely. He called me Radha. He teased me by carrying me on his hip and heaving me on to his shoulders. During the initial period of our honeymoon, he revealed to me the different ways in which women experienced pleasure. While typing the next day's scoop on the computer with his left hand, he would tickle me with his right.

'I like to see women laugh,' he said. 'I hate women who do not laugh. I detest tears!'

Our flat resounded with my laughter. Different sorts: silent smiles, subdued giggles, tickled sniggers, full-throated chuckles, suffocating guffaws. My eyes would fill up, weary from laughing continuously. When I lay down, tired, his lust would awaken. He would kneel on the ground and kiss my feet and then my hair. In a quiet voice, he would rhapsodize about the beauty of my hair, my eyes and cheeks. He made me lovely with his very gaze, a goddess with his mere touch. Sex was a sacred ritual to Madhav. I remembered his chest—soft and warm like that of a huge bird's. Exhausted, I would lie on his chest like a tulsi leaf, like a feather.

I loved him, heedless of all else. I simply loved. Occasionally, when I met acquaintances or my father's friends, and they threw the question, 'How could you do such a thing, Tulsi?' I would sincerely wonder what else I was supposed to have done. I felt deeply compassionate towards those women who neither loved nor were loved by anyone. I worried about the children born to women who had never known love. I, who had graduated from IIT with record marks, became the handmaiden of Madhav. I washed his clothes with affection, and ironed them with devotion. I cooked his beloved food with reverence. The places where he stood and sat, I cleaned as if they were sacred. I blissfully surrendered to him and he accepted me with compassion.

Madhav used to call home at regular intervals: 'Tulsi, what are you doing? If you have finished cooking, do read for some time. Or else, go out for a bit. Why do you sound tired? Don't you have oranges over there? Make an orange juice for yourself . . .'

I would burst out laughing. 'Just come home early, dear . . .'

'See . . . women are like this. They want to be cosseted all the time.'

'I *was* a good woman once upon a time!'

'Tulsi, I am going to spoil you further . . .'

'Absolutely!' And I would start laughing again.

'Have you kissed all twenty-seven of your girlfriends like this?' I once asked Madhav.

'What if I said yes?'

'I am feeling jealous!'

'No . . . Never be jealous! Lord Krishna loved Arjun because there was no envy in his love—it says so in the Mahabharata.'

'I am your lover, not your compatriot.'

'The Lord abandoned Radha because of her jealousy.'

'Are you saying you will abandon me too?'

'I did not say that.' Madhav sat up straight. 'When you love, life is beautiful. Love me, trust me. Do not doubt this at all. The past and the future do not belong to us. Today, this moment—this is the only reality, and it is everlasting.'

I became dull and dispirited. Madhav kissed my forehead and neck with tenderness. 'Simply love.

Forget everything and just love passionately. Jealousy is irrelevant in love.'

Jealousy was indeed irrelevant. Even on the day when Lily Varghese came half running with her American bags. Barely two months after our marriage. It was a Sunday. Madhav, his mundu hitched halfway, and I, in my nightdress, were dusting the carpets and changing the bed sheets when the bell rang.

I opened the door. Lily pushed me aside, and rushed in, her eyes anguished. Madhav stood like a statue, his head held high, the vacuum cleaner in his hand. Lily pounced on him. She embraced him tightly and burst into tears. As if driven insane, she kissed him hard on his lips, bit him on his cheeks and his chest. 'How could you, how could you?' she muttered hysterically. 'I will not give you up, Madhav! I will never ever give you up to anyone!' she threatened.

Madhav took her in his arms and clasped her to his chest. Concerned, he gently stroked her hair. In a voice brimming with love, he asked: 'Oh Lily, sweet Lily, what's this? What will my wife think? See, she is scared . . . Lily, behave yourself . . . Don't be silly . . .'

I stood frozen, the doormat still in my hand. I recognized the woman: *Madhav's twenty-sixth girlfriend*. Lily was a famous journalist. When she was away in New York on a fellowship, the twenty-seventh girlfriend, a Nepali beauty named Hiranmai, took over possession of Madhav. As Lily quibbled and Madhav consoled her, I picked up the vacuum cleaner with trembling hands and continued to clean the bedroom. But when she hit Madhav hard on his cheeks and chest alternately, I became raving mad.

'Lily, that is my husband!' I intervened.

She looked at me as if throwing down a gauntlet. 'But he has been mine for a much longer time ... You have no clue about the depth of our relationship ... I can hit him, maul him, kick him—do whatever I want. He will suffer anything like a tame dog.'

'That was in the past!' My tone was challenging as well.

She looked at Madhav like a wounded tigress.

Madhav's face took on a solemn expression. 'I had many girlfriends. But I have only one wife—Tulsi.' In a kind voice he added, 'It is better that you leave, Lily.'

I will never forget Lily's face when she heard his words. Madhav smoothed his ruffled hair, and started putting the cushion covers and carpets back in their places. Silence reigned in the room. Lily calmly opened the door and stepped out. Overwhelmed, I sat down heavily on the settee. After confirming that Lily had left, Madhav locked the door and knelt before me. He lifted my feet into his hands and buried his face in them. His long eyelashes stroked my feet. And I melted like butter.

Later, he took me to bed. 'Please don't be sad,' he implored. Though I felt like crying, I smiled. He made me sleep and then left our home. Afterwards he called up to inquire if I was feeling better. He returned rather late that night and, holding me close, slept contentedly.

In that dingy brown room of the Maighar, hemmed in by chipped walls replete with numerous cracks, as I lay on the rusty cot beneath the sodden, smelly clothes hanging on the clothes line, I could hear the waves of my old laughter. It was the laughter of a stupid girl who had the arrogance of having found her man.

Later, much later, after Unni and Kanna were born, I had met Lily again. By then several other women had streamed into Madhav's life—a young actress, a lady politician, a writer, a television anchor and, finally, a dancer—and I had come to realize that jealousy was indeed irrelevant.

'I am feeling so sad for you,' Lily had sympathized.

'Why on earth?' I had retorted, stung by false pride.

'Tulsi, you don't deserve so much punishment.'

The sincerity in her voice had made me weak.

'I knew that this would happen,' she continued. 'Do you remember the day I came to your home? After asking me to leave, Madhav left the house himself, two hours or so later . . .? Perhaps you've forgotten, Tulsi.'

'No.'

'He had come to my hotel room. He fell at my feet and begged for forgiveness. He washed my feet with his tears.'

Lily's words had pierced my heart like sharp iron nails.

'He made love to me,' she went on. 'Then he called you from the phone in my room. I was half asleep when I heard him ask, "Are you all right, Tulsi?" I threw him out of my life that day.'

She wiped her tears.

'What can be done? No one can hate him . . . He is simply irresistible.'

'Thank you for the information.'

'Be bold,' she said. 'Please do not hesitate to ask for help . . .'

I had struggled hard to maintain my dignity before her. *The dignity of a doormat.* She affectionately patted the cheeks of Kanna, who was perched on my hip. I was proud of myself for not breaking down in front of her. I felt the same pride when I secured a place for myself in Vrindavan's annadanam queue for the first time, and again when I was summoned at night by a priest of the Rangji temple two days after that.

The room that I was summoned to was in a quarter meant for priests. The man moistened his thick lips repeatedly as he approached me.

'Tulsi, you are such a fine girl. I do not like the idea of you living amidst all these tonsured women . . . You can stay in my home, if you wish. That means with all the facilities. See, my wife is old. As for me, I am not ageing at all . . . I still have enough youth to satisfy a woman like you . . .'

His red satin dhoti, the saffron shawl covering his upper body, the long tilak on his forehead, those thick lips with the snake-like tongue flicking in and out—all of these provoked utter revulsion in me. He was fondling himself as he talked to me. I felt like vomiting. Yet, I also felt a cruel sense of satisfaction. When he touched me, I sincerely wanted to oblige him. But my body had turned to stone.

'You are pretty,' he muttered, licking his lips again.

I started laughing.

'Why are you laughing?'

'Shouldn't women laugh?' I asked him. 'Don't you know that you have to make a woman laugh before you fuck her?'

I had laughed again when he undressed himself. On seeing his flat nose, his protruding tummy and shrivelled organ, I had laughed without stopping.

'Why are you laughing like this? Are you mocking this old man?' He was upset.

'Do not get angry,' I told him gently. 'You can rape me if you want.'

Fed up, the old man had let me go. I too was bitterly frustrated.

My body was full of poison. Love's poison. I did not desire to die. I wanted to survive. To live on, like a horrendous, festering wound. Those who saw me ought to feel this pain. Like Madhav's love, I too should corrode everything around me.

When the midnight puja bells of the Madan Mohan temple rang out, I stretched out on the iron cot in the Maighar. I was curious about Madhav. Had he suffered a heart attack? *Madhav's heart,* I thought facetiously. *Madhav, who could corrode lips while kissing.* As I lay thinking, Ramakrishna Pandit called my name from outside: 'Tulsi mai!'

My heart stopped beating for a moment. I was afraid that he had come to give me some news of Madhav. My hatred for Madhav was all-consuming. I wished to smash him into smithereens. And yet I also wished that he would live on. I wanted his beating heart—so that *I* could corrode it myself. I stepped out of the room. It was a moonlit night. In the dim light, I saw Madhav in the distance. Wrapped in his Kashmiri shawl, he was waiting by Ramakrishna Pandit's side. I was enraged.

The pandit stepped forward, the beam from his torch lighting the way.

'He walked out from the hospital without permission, Tulsi mai. It seems he has something to say to you. He will leave soon after that.'

I stood motionless. I watched Madhav's face as if through a sleepy haze. He had greyed a bit. Lost some hair. Grown a beard. The grey strands gleamed silver in the moonlight, as did the long lashes that framed his large eyes. I stared at Madhav as if he was a stranger. He hobbled towards me, one side of his body drooping. With great effort, he knelt on the ground. Before I realized what was happening, he put his lips, moist and warm, on my feet. My filthy, scarred, calloused feet. I stepped back as if burned. Madhav toppled over, losing balance.

I ran back to my room and fell on to the iron cot, struggling for breath.

From the grimy walls surrounding me, numerous Krishnas in different postures gazed soulfully at me. I went mad. Someone played the flute right in my ears without stopping. I felt like running wildly through the streets, stark naked.

'A flute note by the riverside! Ah, my shattered heart, what is the relevance of recognition now?'

But my legs did not move. I curled up on that iron cot, sheltering in its cold, breathing heavily. My feet felt heavy. It was as if Madhav's lips had fused on to them. I rubbed one foot against the other, hoping to obliterate his touch. I did not succeed. I even tried briskly rubbing an old rag on my feet. Finally, I went to the bathroom and, taking water from the dirty, paan-stained, phlegm-soiled washbasin, washed my feet again and again. It was useless. The flesh and the bones had both corroded away. He still had the capacity to dissolve me.

FOUR

Madhav was like a rich dessert. Women devoured him like ants. I was reduced to destitution within the first three years of our marriage. I discovered a glass barrier between us. When we touched each other with our lips, when our heartbeats merged, the barrier remained between us. He seemed encased in armour even when he undressed himself. Even when we made love, he was searching for someone else in the distance.

It was too late by the time I realized that my understanding as a bride had been wrong—the notion that I was the twenty-eighth and *final* lover who was entering his bedroom. By then I had lost everything. First, my mother—she had died, hardly one month after my elopement. My father lost his sense of judgement. Even before Mallika could finish her MBBS degree, he married her off to the first available doctor. Her dream of becoming an IAS officer was destroyed. In another hastily arranged marriage, eighteen-year-old Tamara, who had scored the second rank in the All India Engineering Entrance Examination, was offloaded on to a businessman thirteen years her senior. A few years later, when I met her in Kochi during the wedding of a minister's son, Tamara had looked at me with hatred. 'I do not want to see you. You destroyed your life as well as ours,' I remembered her accusation now as I lay in the old room in the Maighar.

The honeymoon had ended abruptly. From the lower drawer of the wardrobe in the bedroom, where Madhav stored his documents, a steady procession of corpse-eating ants had marched out. That was the first indication. I was pregnant with Unni at that time. The ants bit me hard when I passed that way unseeingly. Wincing in pain, I had opened the drawer to pull out the papers. That's when I discovered the sweet that had attracted the ants. I was horror-struck! It was a black snake with a half-swallowed rat in its mouth. In spite of knowing that both creatures were dead, I was terrified.

More than the shock of finding a snake in a ninth-floor flat, or the intense distress of seeing it dead in the act of eating the rat, it was the sight of the ants feasting on both—the predator and the prey— that traumatized me. The rotten stench had quickly spread through the flat. I vomited several times. Finally, gathering the putrefied bodies in a plastic bag, I took the elevator down to dump it inside the communal waste bin. When I returned to our flat, I had wept for a long time, without any reason.

That was a strange day. Madhav had gone abroad for a week with the prime minister's entourage. I tried to forget my perturbation by walking around the flat, taking a stroll outside it and visiting an acquaintance in a neighbouring flat.

At night, I listlessly browsed through the loose papers I had retrieved from the drawer. They were letters. 'My dearly beloved,' was how the first letter began. Unable to control my agitation, I paced in the flat, walking in and out of each room. Love weakens humans—makes them fragile and pliable. I did not have the strength to read the letters. Nor did I have the strength not to read them. With a trembling hand, I flipped through them. The first one was from Hiranmai. Below hers was Lily Varghese's letter, and beneath that letters from Susmita Patil, Rakhi Menon, Seema Kashyap, Rasina Shah, Isabella George, Lina Patel, Isha Agrawal, Aruna Balachandran, Saraswati Iyer, Mumtaz Begum, Vimala Panjikaran . . .

Each letter was a reply to Madhav. Each had similar sentences. It was clear that he had written the same lines to them—the very same that he had once written to me. My pride drained away slowly. I had started seething: *Who am I to Madhav? Another woman. The twenty-eighth one. What is it that I am searching for in him? Why did I elope with him? Why did he make me his wife? Was there ever a woman whom he loved truly?*

When he returned, Madhav had burst out laughing upon seeing my reddened eyes and puffy face. He lifted me in his arms and laughingly spun me in the air. Ardently kissing my breasts and neck, he mock-threatened me, saying that the punishment for the doubting Thomas would be special. My suspicions and peeves melted away like butter.

Yet, whenever I happened to meet any of Madhav's ex-girlfriends, the flaming desire in their eyes unnerved me. They were of all varieties: dark, fair, slim, voluptuous; college girls, young women, ladies approaching middle age. When he met these women during dinners or in public places, Madhav would treat them with utmost respect—just as he treated me. He would gaze deeply into their eyes and lovingly caress them. At times, he made them burst out laughing; at others he patiently listened to their problems. My heart would break in despair. But jealousy was irrelevant, of course. Complaints were out of place.

Whenever I attempted to broach the topic, Madhav would ridicule me.

'Tulsi, you are a sadist,' he had said to me one day. 'You know very well that I am yours and yours alone . . . Those women are unloved . . . poor creatures . . .'

'I don't understand you . . .'

Madhav pulled me close and kissed my cheek passionately, even as he continued to drive the car.

'You are pretending that you do not understand . . . I am yours . . . I belong to you physically, emotionally, legally . . . My child is growing in your womb. Why these frivolous doubts then?'

An extraordinary heaviness began weighing down my heart. An iron block seemed to be incessantly choking my breath. I would wake up, drenched in sweat, from a recurring nightmare: Women with heavy bottoms—like corpse-eating ants that walked on two legs—were all over Madhav. Love silenced me and left me helpless.

Years later, corpse-eating ants bit me again. It was my first night at the Maighar. The iron cot had an occupant, an old woman from Bengal named

Padmalata. She was ninety-five years old. When I entered the room she was asleep. Nabaneeta had muttered something unintelligible about her dozing constantly. I had slept in the tiny space between the cots of the two old women, lying on a piece of sackcloth. Sometime in the night, I felt something crawling all over me. I had woken Nabaneeta. Scolding me, she retrieved a matchbox from under her pillow and lit a kerosene lamp. In the yellow light of the lamp, I was astounded by the great spiritual journey of the ants—marching like naked Digambara sadhus—towards Padmalata's nose.

Later, I appropriated the empty cot—a widow's cot, one that has rusted entirely and which hurts the body all over. As I lay on it, the narrow room closed in about me. From amidst the dirt on the wall different Krishnas smiled at me. The room had the stench of a birthing chamber. Who would have given birth to a child in such a room with its hanging calendar of the butter-eating Krishna? The realization struck me afterwards. The excruciating smell was that of death, not birth. It felt as though a dead woman was always lying next to me.

'That is the problem with Vrindavan, beti . . . Krishna never lets go of women . . .' Nabaneeta had laughed, as if she was sharing a joke. But there was vengeance in her laughter too.

'These women return, even after being buried . . . He knows the way to summon them . . . Shameless creatures! If he laughs, they join him . . . If he condescendingly bestows a caress, carried away in that ecstasy they will do anything dirty for him.'

Filling the vacancy left by Padmalata, Chameli bai had come to the room.

'Radha mai or Meera mai?' she had asked on our first meeting. I'd stared at her, wondering.

'In Vrindavan, married women and virgins are Radha mais. Widows are Meera mais.'

'I do not wish to be Radha,' I had hissed with malice. 'I want to be Meera . . . Radha is just one among the sixteen thousand and eight . . . Meera is matchless, the one and only . . .'

I felt good about myself. No, I did not want to be Radha. Had she any relevance outside Seva Kunj? But Meera was not like that. On every path she had traversed, her footsteps lingered, engraved as poems.

'You who seduce me with your sweet words, I will tell everybody that secret! I will beat my drum and reveal it to the world . . .'

'You poor thing!' Nabaneeta's emaciated body shook as she laughed bitterly. 'Open your eyes and look around—everyone you see is a Meera. Those who ran away from the luxurious palaces of their husbands for love, those who wandered insane through the streets . . . Thief, brute—all women are the same to Krishna. He will steal any woman's clothes, eat anyone's butter . . . I am telling you, do not worship him! Beat him off if he comes near you . . . He will pretend to be in love with you, utter sweet words to entice you . . . He will kiss you slyly . . . Beti, he just wants your body. Only your body.'

She became breathless. Then she curled up and slept, dazed with opium. Chameli had observed her indifferently. She revealed that Nabaneeta's lover had abandoned her at Kashi. Many men had abused her before she finally reached Vrindavan. So, Nabaneeta hated all men.

'What about you, mai?'

'Me?'

She pulled away her pallu and revealed the horrid scar across her skinny breasts.

'See, the wound of Partition . . . I was trying to escape. I had lost everything. Everyone. Husband, children, goats, cows, everything . . .'

A tremor crept into her voice. She said that most of the aged women were refugees who had crossed over the border. They had never tried to return.

'If one remembered that journey, there was no going back, beti. You saw just one wound. Beneath it beats a heart with a thousand wounds. To be taken by a man without a touch of love—what could cause a more grievous wound, beti?'

I imagined a man whose face was flushed with love while having sex. Once again poison simmered within my veins.

Chameli bai grinned toothlessly at me. 'Who are you thinking of, my girl? How angry you look!'

'My enemy,' I had muttered.

'Enemy? There is nobody like that. Whatever you see is not what you actually see . . . Everything is maya. Illusion . . . Look at the ants. They ate away Padma's body. Then what happened? Did they turn into Padmalata? No. And when they had finished eating her did Padmalata turn into an ant? No.'

I gazed at her steadily. The image of Madhav surrounded by pretty ants flashed in my memory. I stared quietly at the dirty walls and counted the different Krishnas on them. The butter-eating Krishna resembled Kanna. Balaram reminded me of Unni.

Twelve years. I had spent every single day like an ant, eating away into my memories. I would rush to the bhajanmandap after the daily morning bath in the Yamuna. There I would shout out in a frenzy: 'Hare Rama Hare Rama, Rama Rama Hare Hare, Hare Krishna Hare Krishna, Krishna Krishna Hare Hare.'

Like the black ants that crawl all over sweets, dark, unsightly women with their heads tonsured surrounded the Radha Krishna statue. Just like the animals in a slaughterhouse, these ten thousand women too had marks on their foreheads. They had been discarded by fathers, lovers, husbands. Refugees. Orphans. The ten thousand girlfriends of Krishna. Sometimes I felt like laughing. I could often feel my madness stirring as I sang the bhajans. Then I would recall the paths I had travelled. The roads I had walked on. The school where I had studied, wearing a blazer and tie. College, where life had been a riot of colours. The professional college, where I had gained admission after a tough entrance examination. How many lessons I had mastered in my short lifespan! And yet, in the end, I repeat only four lines.

Those days the room rent was five rupees. The allowance was ten rupees. A big amount indeed! In the mornings, I purchased flowers for a rupee and offered them at the deserted Govind Dev temple. That temple is similar to my love. Useless and empty. It is a place where female monkeys prowl, with babies hanging from their stomachs.

I would think of my children—of the nights when I had conceived them. I would remember Madhav—his eyes, his honeyed words, his betrayal. My body was dead. The single throb of life in it was my malicious hatred for him. One day, my retribution would be complete. He would come to me with filth all over his body. I would dip him in the dark Yamuna of my vengeance. I would wash away the memories of my children.

Life had taken a decisive turn after Unni was born. I was a happy woman when he was conceived. Madhav had steadily risen in his profession. Money was abundant; we had status and prestige. Madhav's handsome pictures appeared regularly in trendy magazines. I had given birth to Unni in Kerala. Madhav's mother had looked after me. She was a simple woman. She spoke with great pride about Madhav's father. He had died when she was pregnant. She had given birth as a widow. Madhav had grown up without a father. When she told me all that, I realized how little I knew about Madhav; it was upsetting. The things I did not know outnumbered what I knew.

'I do not know anything about you,' I had complained to him one day.

'Don't know anything about me? Don't you know that I have a mole on my chest? That I have a scar on my thigh?'

'Yes. And that you have had twenty-seven lovers. But . . .'

'But?' Madhav had queried, sounding peeved. 'Tulsi, you should not hurt me like this. There is nothing in my life that is unknown to you.'

I had swallowed my grievances. I simply could not bear to hurt him. How could I do that to someone who gave me such joy?

When I returned after childbirth, the kitchen and the drawing room had looked unfamiliar, as if they belonged to some other house.

'My friend and his wife had stayed over for some time,' Madhav had explained. As I was cleaning, I discovered a black brassiere underneath the cot in the second bedroom. When I asked him about it, he hugged me close and kissed me, feigning hurt. 'You are the mother of my child . . . Yet you doubt me . . .'

He always stopped my questions with his kisses. He trounced me with sweetened words. I forgot all my misgivings when he showered me with kisses and tickled me, and soothed me with his mellifluous voice. Yet the glass barrier between us grew thicker. Meanwhile, Madhav shifted from newspaper journalism to television. His popularity grew. He began to return home at unearthly hours. He would play with the baby hurriedly. He would kiss me hastily. Our conversations became a mere ritual. I waited hours on end for him, rocking my child's cradle. I washed his clothes and cooked his food. Some days, I lost my cool and became harsh. When I displayed my bitterness, instead of picking a fight, he shut my lips with his kisses. However, slowly he became more and more distant. To avoid future confrontations, he became extremely busy.

When I called him, he would say: 'Tulsi, I am busy. I'll call you later.' When I tried to speak, he would interrupt with: 'Not now, let me finish some work.' When it was time for bed, he would say: 'I have a headache, you go to sleep.' From dawn to late night, until he returned, I waited for him. As soon as he woke up, he became busy with incessant phone calls. He would head out immediately after breakfast. He would return very late at night. With a yawn, he would slip into bed, exhausted. I would lie by his side, burning slowly. I needed his love. I ached for the caress of his soft palm. I craved the sound of his sweet nothings in my ears. My body desired his touch. I yearned for him with my entire being; with all of a woman's longing. But Madhav ignored me totally. He pretended to be unaware of my desires. When I complained, he would drop a kiss—as if giving me alms. When I expressed my annoyance and nagged him, he would get ready for sex as if making a compromise. Our love became a forgotten vessel of milk left upon the fire. Soon the milk boiled and spilled over, leaving the vessel empty.

I prowled about inside my home, extremely disturbed. I constantly chattered with Unni as I worked in the kitchen. I spoke about my life. My dreams. My foolishness. 'Your mother has no one, Unni.' As he lay on his back, moving his little feet and hands, I had looked at my baby pleadingly. 'Love me when you grow up. That love should be true. It should be real. Don't betray your mother. Don't cheat her with lies.' He sobbed when he heard that. He had a cleft in his chin, just like Madhav. Yet when I looked at his face, I saw my own. He had inherited my suspicious eyes.

Desolation blew around us constantly, like a winter wind. We froze like corpses.

One day, inside the drawer of a table, I saw a financial statement about a huge amount taken as a loan at exorbitant interest rates.

'Oh, that is for the television channel. It is official,' said Madhav.

Two days later there was a piece of gossip in a film magazine—about Madhav giving fifteen lakh rupees to an actress. It became a heavy weight in my heart. I did not question Madhav about it. That was not an easy task. The glass barrier had turned into a granite wall. Four years passed by in this manner. Occasionally he came into the bedroom with an apologetic smile. Ignoring my resistance, he would have sex with me. My heart wept when he touched me. After coitus, we would move apart; he with a yawn, and I, with tears.

I often remembered Vinay with a deep sense of regret in those days. *If I see him, I should fall at his feet. I should wash his feet with my tears. But I hope I do not see him.*

Yet I did. It was during a dinner party, after Vinay had transferred to the Delhi office of his American company. Out on the lawn, I was sitting alone at a table in the corner. Some distance away, Madhav was

K.R. Meera

tenderly stroking the plump back of a middle-aged
ex-girlfriend. A worm crawled along my spine.

Vinay had approached as I was taking my second
glass of vodka.

'Remember me?' he asked.

I sat there with the words drying up in my mouth.
He had put on some weight. There were dark circles
beneath his eyes. Pulling out a chair, he sat down
next to me. Seeing the ex-girlfriend resting against
Madhav's chest and sharing her sorrows, Vinay
quipped in a sad tone, 'Tulsi, you have indeed become
modern.' I felt as embarrassed as I would have if
someone had stolen my clothes.

Later, Vinay visited the flat. He observed with
pity the life I had—sullied in just six years. I conversed
with him, trying to hide my acute discomfiture. But
when I learned that he was still unmarried I cried.

'Forgive me,' I pleaded.

Vinay removed his glasses, and wiped his tears. 'It
does not matter . . . but I expected to find you living
very happily . . . I wanted to see that . . .'

'I do not know what to do, Vinay . . .'

'Try applying for a job . . .'

After Vinay had left, I sat beside my sleeping
son. I imagined being married to Vinay. I might

have earned a name as a scientist. I would have lived without any troubles. Perhaps Vinay would not have kissed me like Madhav did. But he would never have caressed other women in my presence. He would never have driven me to drink. Who knew, after all? Maybe, even then, I would have remained dissatisfied. A different sort of dissatisfaction, perhaps.

I reflected on my life: on my higher education, my career, and the life that I should have lived. A stench arose from that imagery—as though from soured milk. A sigh emerged from my heart. Like a poisonous flame, it scalded my chest. It seemed to me that a devastated woman's grief-stricken sigh had the potential to burn down a house. However, on reaching Vrindavan, I realized my mistake. Had my surmise been right, Vrindavan would have turned into a city of ashes a long time ago.

My stubborn pride had not let me kiss Vinay's feet that day. That became possible only in Vrindavan. I met him unexpectedly. It was the day after Madhav had kissed my feet. I was prancing along the road near Nidhivan, singing a Meera bhajan.

'I have never stolen anything that belonged to another. I have never hurt anyone either. Then why do

you scorn me so? Do you expect me to sit astride a donkey after alighting from an elephant?'

I was singing it without any tune or rhythm. I felt light-headed, as if I was drunk.

It was then that Vinay had stuck his head out of the car and called, 'Tulsi!' I was taken aback. As he emerged from the car, my pallu slipped, exposing my shaven head. A herd of goats hurried past through the space between us. I smiled, hiding my uneasiness. Vinay tried hard not to look at me. He removed his glasses and resolutely dried his eyes. Behind him, from the Govind Dev temple, a group of green parrots took flight. The temple had been emptied of its riches by Aurangzeb's robbery. Now it was a place where bats, rats and darkness dwelled. I remembered the inside of that temple. Innumerable vermin. Countless corpse-eating ants.

'Tulsi, I cannot bear to see this.' Vinay wept.

I looked at him. I grinned sympathetically, revealing my toothless gums. Then, kneeling on that path, spattered as it was with goat shit, cow dung, spit and urine, I touched my forehead to his feet.

'Tulsi!' came the anguished cry.

'I am not Tulsi. Meera. Meera mai . . .'

'Madhav regrets deeply,' said Vinay. 'Tulsi, please forgive him.'

'Who needs Gangajal after dying of thirst?'

'Please come with me ... Let us talk about this.'

'There is only one man in Meera's Vrindavan. The rest are all women . . .' And then I yelled out furiously, 'Bolo Krishna Krishna jai!'

I ran towards the Govind Dev temple, without looking back at Vinay. As I ran, I sang, as if I had gone insane.

'My Lord raised the Govardhan; that was really easy; did he not rouse my body?'

I haughtily begged in front of the Govind Dev temple till evening. When the stars started crawling over the sky like ants, I rose from there. I walked back with my empty begging bowl. Tomorrow, I decided, I will get into a scuffle with the monkeys. They will clamber over me like ants.

I needed wounds. To hurt myself more grievously, I needed more wounds.

FIVE

Love was like the demoness Putana. It applied poison to its nipples and wore the guise of Lalita. It hugged me close to its bosom too. While giving milk to Kanna, my body had grown weak. He was one and a half years old. Unni was five.

As I massaged Chameli's back in the Maighar that night, I remembered another cold November night.

Chameli struggled to breathe, her asthma aggravated by the approaching new moon eve. I ministered to her, forgoing my sleep.

'Why don't you go away, beti?' she asked me, gasping. 'Your relatives have come, have they not?'

'She will not leave,' Nabaneeta said snarkily, consuming opium. 'That thief Krishna, he will not let her go.'

I smiled, exposing the gaps of my lost teeth: 'Mai, I shall merge into this place. My Lord lives here.' My Lord! Lord of the sixteen thousand and eight. I felt a grudging affection for Banke Bihari. *How very mischievous of him!* What could be naughtier than summoning Madhav and Vinay to Vrindavan with his flute?

'*Oh, doesn't the Cloud-coloured One—he who plays with both life and death—know Meera's rage?*'

My rage.

I recalled Vinay's request. *Forgive Madhav.* I felt like laughing. Another experiment of love. What a variety of experiments! I remembered the time when I had been pregnant with Kanna. Madhav had stopped coming to the flat. Money was running low; I had to struggle even to manage household expenses. When he was absent for two weeks at a stretch, I visited his office, my pregnancy at full term then. It was a pathetic journey. One child inside me, one child holding my hand. Self-confidence is the esteem one feels about oneself. But as I sat in the reception area of his television network, all my self-esteem drained away. The topper from IIT Chennai and beloved daughter of the inspector general was dead. I waited there, full of self-loathing. I was nothing but an unattractive, indiscreet, abandoned woman.

Madhav, wearing a new coat, had entered the room smartly. He was appalled for a moment. Then, with a hastily pasted-on smile, he asked why I was there and why I had not bothered to call instead. He gave some vague reasons for not coming home, as if offering an explanation to an acquaintance or distant relative. He blamed his busy schedule and his workload for his inability to call me. Mumbling something, he casually patted Unni. I listened quietly. With no semblance of anger, I smiled at him.

'What should I do, Madhav? Return home to Kerala?'

Madhav had grinned, slightly disconcerted. That grin had torn away at my pride. This was not the man I had loved. That had been someone else. The man before me was a total stranger. My eyes stung with unshed tears. But I did not cry. Unni had walked by my side, his head lowered, holding on tightly to my hand. The sight of his crestfallen face had crushed me.

I wrote to my father for the first time since I had eloped. A single line: 'Your daughter Tulsi seeks forgiveness, falling at your feet.'

My father had arrived by my side as soon as he received my letter. He took us back home with him. Madhav's calls began after that. 'Where have you kept my razor, Tulsi? My towel? My shirts? Trousers? Coats? Which coat should I wear with the ash-coloured shirt, Tulsi? You have misunderstood me. The truth is very different. Your suspicions debilitate me. Just be sure of one thing. I have no life without you or my children. You are my strength.'

He said the words I had been thirsting to hear. My heart was consoled. *Nothing had happened really*, I told myself. *Madhav could never be deceitful. I am not just another woman to him.*

I started seeing him wherever I looked. My eyes would fill with tears when I was alone. The rock in my heart became doubly heavy. The veins of my heart were stretched to their limit, and I thought they would explode. *He loves me*, I argued with myself. I laid down the evidence to justify this. Yet sometimes, I wondered: *What is this love that a man is supposed to have for a woman?* That alone, remained beyond my comprehension.

Madhav had flown in when I gave birth to Kanna. He had burst into tears, embracing Unni. He played with Kanna, who was his exact replica. He kissed me and asked for forgiveness. He told me that he could not sleep without seeing the baby. He mocked at all my suspicions. He took us back to Delhi with him. And life began to be eaten away by ants, just like before.

I tried not to think about Madhav. He was the children's father. A man who came back from work in the evening, and left again in the morning. Having removed love's poisonous fangs, forcefully using pincers, I fastened it inside a basket and hid it under a cot. I prowled restlessly around the house.

But, one afternoon, when I was giving Kanna his baby meal, *she* walked in. The television anchor. She had burst into tears. Apparently Madhav had got involved with a famous dancer. I had listened with indifference. But when I heard about her conceiving a child and being forced to abort it, I felt the beginnings of a mad turbulence within.

'Yet, I cannot hate him,' she had wept.

I had smiled dryly. 'I can understand . . .'

'I will never be able to think of another man again . . .'

'No one can do that . . .'

After she left, I had felt lifeless. Mine was a life that had been annihilated. *Why did he destroy me?* I contemplated that question very seriously. *How had I wronged him? What had those thirty-two other women done to him?*

I had fought bitterly with Madhav that night. He hated women who fought. He disliked women who raised their voices. Women should stay beautiful. They should always be smiling. I could never smile again.

'Why did you destroy that girl?' I asked him.

He had looked at me with utter revulsion: '*I?* Destroy *her? She* was using me! Listen, Tulsi, she was the one who betrayed me.'

I looked at Kanna, asleep in his cradle. 'Like him, another Kanna.'

Madhav had something in his hand. He threw it down with great force. 'I hate you,' he shouted. 'My peace of mind disappears the moment I enter this house! Continuous fault-finding, constant suspicions. You are sick! What the hell do you know about a man? You think I will spend all my time pampering you? Look, Tulsi, be practical! No man can ever confine himself to a single woman. That's the way men are built.'

'What about women?' I asked.

'That's different. You are genetically tuned . . . I am bloody fed up.'

'Me too.'

'Let us separate.'

The word 'separation' felled me; as if I had been hit right on the head. I thought about it. Separation from Madhav. Then what? I imagined returning to my father's home. A child in either hand. Exhausted body. Sunken eyes. A life, gathering ants, caught between my sisters' lives and that of my father. Perhaps I would get a job. Earn a salary. Bring up my children. But all for what? In the wake of Madhav's rejection, what relevance did Tulsi and her two children have in this world? What significance remained in the body that had been purified with love?

I was not a woman who had merely pretended to love in order to make a living. I had sacrificed everything for love. After he left the house with his belongings, I tried to add and subtract, in an attempt to rewrite my life. But it was difficult to forget Madhav. Difficult for the wounds to heal. When I opened a newspaper, I would see his name.

When I switched on the television, I would see his face.

He came back in November.

'I want to tell you something. I am in deep trouble.'

'Tell me.'

'Bhama wants me to marry her ...'

'Ah.'

'I cannot make a decision, Tulsi.'

I laughed.

'No one will love me the way you do,' he said. 'The negative publicity of the divorce will affect me too.'

'Still, you cannot give her up.'

'Tulsi, she is not like you. Famous dancer! An extraordinary genius—'

I went berserk. 'An extraordinary genius is she!' I grabbed him by his collar. 'Was I not one too? I, who passed with record marks from IIT—was I not extraordinary too? I gave up everything for you. Then what happened? What do I have today? My children and I, we subsist on my father's kindness. Get the hell out! Get the hell away from me!'

Two days later, Vinay came to see me. 'What is all this?' he asked. 'Madhav wants me to persuade you to give him a divorce.'

I had laughed so uproariously that my eyes had filled with tears.

'Tulsi, relax,' Vinay said softly.

'Okay, I'll do it,' I said.

'What will you do afterwards?' Vinay inquired.

'What can I *not* do, afterwards?' I had laughed again.

That night, after drinking vodka, I called up Madhav. 'Come to a restaurant with Bhama tomorrow. We will settle everything then.'

'See, Tulsi, please do not hurt her.'

'Why?'

'I did not want to upset you. But then, not telling you would be a betrayal. Listen, she is pregnant . . .'

'Congratulations!'

I hung up. My pride had not let me cry. So I had struggled to smile. I hugged and kissed my children. I tickled them, and made them laugh. My body burned. Shivered. Burning tears sprang from my eyes. I again kissed my children soundly.

My man. He was going to be a father once more.

My lips twisted as a sob broke. Unni and Kanna stared at me in wonder. I gave them a bath in the morning, and dressed them in new clothes.

I purchased toys for them. We played in the park. When we came home, we played camping. Then, I gave them milk.

Kanna was a bonny baby. He had Madhav's large eyes and long eyelashes. He always smiled sweetly like Madhav. As he sipped the poisoned milk, he twitched his nose. I had told them the story of Putana, my voice trembling strangely. He had drunk the milk listening to the tale. He had hiccuped a bit, showing signs of mild discomfort. A little later, he began to sweat. Yawning widely, Kanna had leaned against my breast. He had sucked his thumb, and looked into my eyes with his own large ones. His eyelashes had slowly collapsed like the leaves of a touch-me-not plant. My body had become a void as I laid him in the cradle. Next, I called Unni to my side. He drank the milk without any questions. 'Bitter,' had been his only complaint and I had added more sugar. That, as I mentioned earlier, had been the month of November. It was a night with bitterly chilly winds.

I lay down with Unni and Kanna, hugging them to my chest. I think I must have wept. I told them about a lot of things. About the world, about life. About those days when I had carried them inside me. About their father. About the unending love I had for Madhav. My dead children. Their bodies slowly cooled, resting against the warmth of mine. Kanna was sucking his thumb even then. Blood dripped from his mouth, rolling down his chubby hand. I kissed my baby son again. 'We cannot give up, my children. We have to defeat your father. We have to leave him before he can abandon us. We have to purify your father with the pain of separation too.'

Later, I locked the door and went out. I met Madhav and Bhama in the garden restaurant of a five-star hotel. I smiled openly. I welcomed them like a new couple of my acquaintance. I offered them sweets. Madhav sat with his head bowed. Bhama tried to smile, flustered and uncomfortable. Madhav looked good in his white T-shirt and grey trousers. Wearing a yellow kurta decorated all over with gems and pearls, Bhama looked very beautiful too. I looked at her with resentment. A perfect figure. A lovely face. He would love her like he had loved me. He would make her laugh with his jokes. When she grew tired from laughter, his lust would stir. His kisses. His eyes with those long eyelashes. His chest, warm like a bird's.

My heart beat harder. *I should not have loved him so intensely. I should not have depended on him to this extent. No one should love* anyone *beyond a limit. I loathe every love story except my own.* I signed on the joint petition for divorce with vengeance. Although I tried to control it, a deep sigh escaped me. They got up to leave.

'I shall leave for Kerala tomorrow. Madhav, please drop me home, if you can,' I said.

'Sure,' Madhav said.

'Bhama, you need not bother.' I looked at her with compassion.

In the car I spoke about air travel and the climate. Eager to help me, Madhav found out the flight timings for the next day and informed me accordingly. I thought about our lives together. *The laughter I have had. The kisses I have had. My heart and my life—both offered to Madhav. Now, when we are separating, I have become a total nonentity. Empty. No job, no salary, no earnings, no beauty, no health, no laughter even. I will never be able to love anyone again. I will never be able to make anyone happy again.*

When we reached the flat, I said: 'Give me one more night. In the memory of our love.'

Madhav had been stunned. Tears filled his eyes. He became agitated. 'Tulsi, I have sinned against you. I know that. Forgive me!'

'Oh, no! What wrong have you done?' I caressed his cheeks. Undressed him. 'Madhav, you are like Krishna, aren't you? Love incarnate? Like the Krishna of Vrindavan, are you not a slave to love and devotion? . . . Madhav, you do not realize it. You are not in love with any woman. You are in love with love. That is why no woman can ever limit you to herself.'

I embraced his naked body.

'I will never be able to embrace any man again,' I whispered sweetly.

'Tulsi, I am hurting badly.'

'But I am not.'

'The kids will wake up.' He looked at the bed with unease.

'Oh, no! They will not be waking up,' I smiled.

I kissed him. That kiss was no pretence. My intense desire for him was no sham either. He surrendered to me. Made love to me as of old. Caressed me as he once used to. At one point, his eyes filled with tears. He became weak and cowardly.

'Oh God, what have I done to you?' he murmured.

'Don't be silly.' I smiled. 'I am a refugee. I begged for your love. You gave me alms. You can never refuse any woman.'

All night long, we stayed in bed, naked and entwined. I discussed so many things with him. Everything that I could not share in eight years of togetherness, I voiced that night. I had quite a lot to say. How he had never given me enough time, had always been busy! On that last night, though the poisonous fangs had long been removed, the hood of my love reared high. We mated like two serpents. After our lovemaking, we separated—I, laughing, and he, sobbing.

Inside my head, something ineffable flashed and turned, like the serpent Kaliya himself. The poison made me ecstatic. Towards morning, when he started dozing, I shook him awake. 'Madhav, look, ants!'

He woke up, disgruntled, rubbing his eyes.

I showed him the steady march of the ants. 'Corpse eaters,' I said.

He screamed in horror. I was stark naked. With my long hair flying free, I laughed uproariously. I went round and round the room. The earth went round and round with me. Our king-sized bed turned round and round. The fan, the sofa and the wardrobe that held the love letters from Madhav's girlfriends—all went round and round. The dead bodies of my children, crawling all over with ants, went round and round. Everything, everything went round and round.

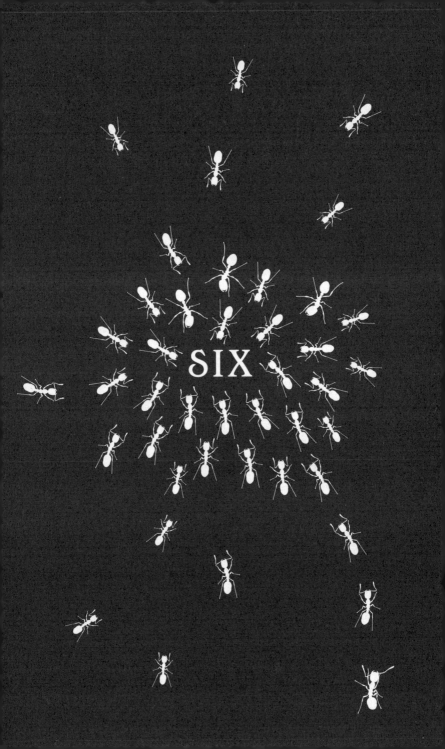

SIX

Love tried to murder me like Putana. It applied poison on her nipples and made me drink her milk. I drank the poison. I drank the milk. Then I drank her blood, furiously. I felt like weeping, looking at Chameli and Nabaneeta as they slept. My breasts were swollen with the milk that had gone waste. I was heartbroken.

In the afternoon, I started off for the Brij Govind Super Speciality hospital. I covered my tonsured head with the loose end of my sari, and climbed up the steps. I approached Madhav's room. He was lying all alone. When he saw me he smiled lovingly. He extended his hands in welcome.

'I knew you would come, Tulsi,' Madhav whispered, 'I knew that.'

I moved silently towards him. I touched the soft palms of his hands with my hardened ones. Hands that had grown hard from washing the clothes of the widows of the Maighar, from cleaning the floors splattered with their urine and phlegm. He looked lovingly at my face with its sunken eyes and toothless gums. In my mind, the faces of each of his lovers started appearing, one by one.

'Let us go back,' Madhav said. 'I have no one else but you.'

I remembered my children then. My children, who had lain dead—their faces twisted, the younger one still sucking his thumb. *My children*. I laughed.

'It's true, Tulsi, I have no one else.' he said. 'The day you left me, everything ended. Bhama abandoned me. Tulsi, I am afraid of women now. I suffered from a stroke. I lost control of one side of my body.'

I laughed and laughed. It exhausted me. Unable to control my laughter, I left the room. I continued laughing as I descended the steps, as I purchased fruits worth ten rupees from the shop at the front of the Govind Dev temple. I laughed as I picked up the broom from the watchman's cabin and as I climbed up to the third storey of the temple. I saw Vrindavan beneath me. Dirty and desolate Vrindavan. Temples like graveyards. Monkeys like ants. The defiled Yamuna.

Love is like Putana. Applying poison on her nipples, it will disguise itself as Lalita, and chase you. The Cloud-coloured One waits in the form of darkness amidst the red pillars. A darkness that smelled of bird shit and bats. I threw the fruits on the cold, red marble floor. The monkeys came rushing in. I fought bitterly with them. They surrounded me like ants. They bit me like dogs. Blood flowed from my neck and arms and legs. I laughed as if tickled. As I fell, I remembered Madhav. I remembered my children. I imagined his lovers with tonsured heads, toothless, skinny, with begging bowls, crawling on all fours like ants.

Madhav is mine. I will love him forever. I will love him with malevolence. I will defeat him with love. I will purify him. Then, at last, I will merge into him.

That is how I shall end this story. The autobiography of a Meera sadhu.

On the third storey of the Govind Dev temple, immersed in blood and darkness, I lay, waiting ecstatically for the final merging with the corpse-eating ants.

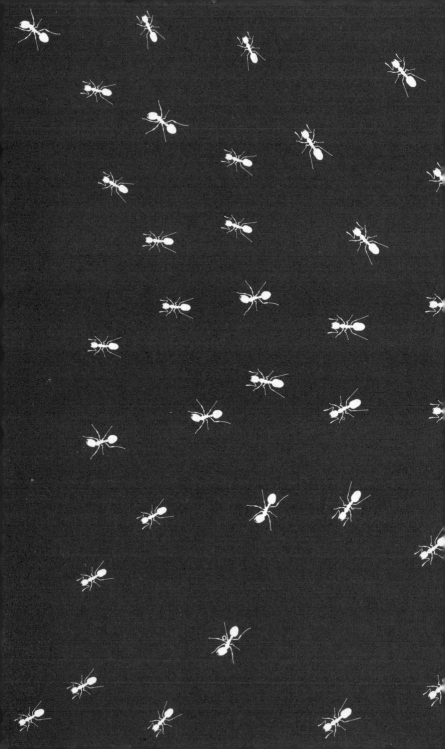

AUTHOR'S NOTE

The Poison of Love is my fifth book daring to transcend the boundaries of Malayalam, the language in which I write and dream.

Right from the publication of *Yellow Is the Colour of Longing*, I have been surprised to find how easily non-Malayali readers relate to my works. They seem to enjoy them as if they are originals, thanks of course to the brilliance of the translators I have been fortunate enough to associate with. I don't have enough words to thank Ministhy S., who has been amazingly invested in this book ever since we met and has worked hard to ensure that this translation sees the light of the day.

Originally titled *Meerasadhu*, this novel has attracted a large number of readers, mostly women, of all age groups. They have come in search of me, to my home, to public meetings, literature festivals, weddings and even funerals, just to tell me how much this book tore at their hearts. Each one claimed that Tulsi's experience mirrored her own. While writing the book, I had imagined that there would be only two or three Tulsis in the world, apart from the sixteenth-century poet Meera Bai. But later, to my horror, I realized that this world has produced and devastated countless Tulsis. Perhaps, every one of us cannot help turning into a Tulsi at some point in our lives.

The most special thing about *The Poison of Love* is that, once again, I have worked with the same wonderful people who were part of *The Gospel of Yudas*. I am immensely thankful to each one of them—my commissioning editor and dear friend Ambar Sahil Chatterjee who made this book possible; Shatarupa Ghoshal, the copy editor who has worked on my last three books; and the brilliant team of Meena Rajasekaran and Ranganath Krishnamani who have created a breathtaking cover for yet another book.

ALSO BY THE SAME AUTHOR

The Unseeing Idol of Light
Translated by Ministhy S.

'An intimate and penetrating portrayal of light and
love. This novel is engrossing and forensic, rich in
complexity and intense in its sadness. K.R. Meera's
prose is always a pleasure, a place where language
becomes landscape'—Meena Kandasamy

One fateful day, Deepti vanishes mysteriously. Baffled by
her disappearance and consumed with grief, Prakash, her
husband, loses his eyesight. For Prakash, the inexplicable
loss of Deepti is doubly painful because she was pregnant
with their child. And no amount of consolation can bring
him solace in the years that ensue.

Into this void steps Rajani, a woman with a tormented
past. Despite her initial disdain of Prakash, she steadily
finds herself drawn to him. And although an intense
desire brings them together, Prakash is unable to give
Rajani the love she craves just as he is powerless to dispel
the luminous memory of Deepti. But where will this
grave obsession lead?

The Unseeing Idol of Light is a haunting tale that explores
love and loss, blindness and sight, obsession and suffering—
and the poignant interconnections between them.

Fiction

ALSO BY THE SAME AUTHOR

The Gospel of Yudas
Translated by Rajesh Rajamohan

'A skilful achievement . . . Lyrical and luminous
prose'—Meena Kandasamy, *The Hindu*

Young and impressionable, Prema is deeply infatuated
with Yudas, the enigmatic man who dredges corpses from
the bottom of the nearby lake. Longing to be rescued
from the tyranny of her father, a former policeman who
zealously tortured Naxalite rebels during the Emergency,
Prema dreams of escape and finds herself drawn to the
Naxal political ideology. Convinced that Yudas was one of
the inmates at her father's prison camp, she believes that
only he can save her. But Yudas is haunted by secrets of his
own, and like his biblical namesake Judas Iscariot, he bears
the burden of crushing guilt.

Ferociously powerful and utterly absorbing, *The Gospel
of Yudas* raises alarmingly relevant questions about the
politics of allegiance and the price of idealism. It is also a
deeply human story about remorse, redemption and love.

'Sucks a reader in with its calm writing only to drown her
in a tidal wave of human honesty'—*Hindustan Times*

'Revolutionary literature'—*India Today*

Fiction

ALSO BY THE SAME AUTHOR

Hangwoman
Translated by J. Devika

'A contemporary masterpiece'—*Mint*

The Grddha Mullick family bursts with marvellous tales of hangmen and hangings in which they figure as eyewitnesses to the momentous events that have shaped the history of the subcontinent. When twenty-two-year-old Chetna Grddha Mullick is appointed the first woman executioner in India, assistant and successor to her father, her life explodes under the harsh lights of television cameras. When the day of the execution arrives, will she bring herself to take a life?

Meera's spectacular imagination turns the story of Chetna's life into an epic and perverse coming-of-age tale. The lurid pleasures of voyeurism and the punishing ironies of violence are kept in agile balance as the drama hurtles to its inevitable climax.

'Meera weaves history, romance and the politics of the present together into a narrative of incredible complexity'—*Caravan*

'Immense, intense ... [with] chillingly clear-eyed vignettes ... [and] moments of razor-sharp dark humour too'—*India Today*

'One of the most extraordinary accomplishments in recent Indian fiction'—*Indian Express*

'A daring book ... Deliciously engrossing'—*The Hindu*

'An epic novel'—*Outlook*

Fiction